Brady Brady
and the Runaway Goalie

Written by Mary Shaw
Illustrated by Chuck Temple

PUBLISHED BY
BRADY BRADY INC.

Published in Canada in 2004 by

Brady Brady Inc.
P.O. Box 367
Waterloo, Ontario
Canada
N2J 4A4

Canadian Cataloguing in Publication Data

ISBN 0-9735557-1-8

Brady helps out when his team's goalie suffers from a
case of nerves and disappears before a big game.

ZAMBONI and the configuration of the Zamboni® ice resurfacing machine
are registered trademarks of Frank J. Zamboni & Co., Inc.

Printed and bound in Canada

Keep adding to your Brady Brady book collection. Make sure you read:

- Brady Brady and the Super Skater
- Brady Brady and the Great Rink
- Brady Brady and the Twirlin' Torpedo
- Brady Brady and the Singing Tree
- Brady Brady and the Big Mistake
- Brady Brady and the Great Exchange
- Brady Brady and the Most Important Game
- Brady Brady and the MVP

For my sister, Erin
Mary Shaw

To my mother, June,
whose encouraging words and actions
have been a source of inspiration
Chuck Temple

Brady loved winter. He loved winter because he loved hockey.
Hockey was all he thought about. He thought about it so much
that everyone had to call him twice to get his attention.
It drove his family *crrraaazy!*

> "Brady, Brady! Is your bed made?"
> "Brady, Brady! Hatrick wants out."
> "Brady, Brady! You're spilling your milk!"

Pretty soon they just called him Brady Brady. It was easier that way.

Brady was on a team called the Icehogs. The rink they played at was right around the corner from Brady's house. It wasn't far, but Brady always left early so he could be the first one there.

One Saturday morning, the Icehogs were playing a nasty team called the Dragoons. The Dragoons were *undefeated*. Brady was excited and a little nervous as he headed to the rink.

On the way in, Brady always said hello to his friend Chester.
Chester was the Icehogs' goalie, and the smartest kid Brady knew.
He often helped Brady with his math.

Chester also helped at the concession stand before every game.
He said munching on popcorn, instead of thinking about flying pucks,
got rid of the butterflies in his stomach.

Brady noticed that Chester looked especially jittery today.
"See you in the dressing room, Chester." Brady waved on his way past.

"Sure, Brady Brady," mumbled Chester, but he did not wave back.

There was usually a lot of chatter before a game,
but today the Icehogs' dressing room was almost silent.
The Dragoons' nasty reputation had the Icehogs worried.

When everyone was dressed, they gathered in the center
of the room for their team cheer. It wasn't quite as loud as usual.

"We've got the power,
We've got the might,
We've got the spirit . . .

. . . Something isn't right!"

They looked around the room . . . and saw a heap of goalie equipment.

Chester was missing!

"Brady Brady! See if you can find him," said the Coach.
Brady rushed away as fast as he could. A second later he was back
holding a note that had been taped to the door.

Brady read it out loud.

"Oh, no!" groaned the Coach. "We can't play without our goalie!"

Some of the kids sat down and began to unlace their skates.
"Wait!" cried Brady. "We *do* have a goalie.
We just have to *find* him."

They checked behind the popcorn machine at the concession stand. No Chester.

They checked under the bleachers. There were blobs of gum stuck to the bottom of the seats, but no Chester.

They checked everywhere — even the girls' washroom.

No Chester.

Finally, they checked the Zamboni garage. There was Chester, on top of the ice machine.

"Come down, Chester. We need you," Brady pleaded with his friend.

"I just can't face the Dragoons, Brady Brady," Chester whimpered. "I'm scared."

"You don't have to face them alone, son," said the Coach. "We're the Icehogs. We stick together."

"We're all a bit nervous, Chester," Brady added. "But you can outsmart the Dragoons any day."

The rest of the Icehogs started to cheer. This time they were as loud and as proud as ever.

"We've got the power,
We've got the might,
Chester's our goalie,
He's all right!"

Chester climbed down from the Zamboni machine.

Out on the rink, the Icehogs lined up against the Dragoons. Brady could hear Chester's teeth chattering behind his mask. The ref dropped the puck and the game began.

The Dragoons tripped and slashed and played a pretty mean game, but the Icehogs didn't give up. They knew they had to play hard and help Chester out — especially since he had his eyes shut most of the time.

When the final buzzer sounded, there was no score.
In overtime no one scored. That meant only one thing . . .
a sudden death shoot-out!

Chester tried to leave the ice, but his teammates dragged him back.

"Come on, Chester, you can do it," Brady said, patting his friend on the back. "You can do anything you put your mind to."

The Icehogs were to go first,
and Brady was picked to shoot.
Starting at center ice, he raced toward
the goalie with the puck on the end of his stick.
He could hear the cheers of his teammates.

Brady fired the puck.
There was a *ping* as it nicked the crossbar — and flew into the net!
The crowd went wild, except for the Dragoons' fans, of course.

It was the Dragoons' turn to shoot. Brady looked at Chester and gave him a thumbs-up. "Remember, Chester, you can do anything you put your mind to!"

The Dragoons player began his charge. Sweat trickled down Chester's face, but he didn't close his eyes. Instead, he began to think.

"The speed of the puck . . . times the arc of the puck . . ."
Chester muttered, ". . . that means it should land . . . *riiight* . . .

. . . HERE!"

Thwack!
The puck landed in
Chester's outstretched glove.

"Holy moly! What a goalie!" the Icehogs hollered.
They jumped over the boards to mob Chester,
who still hadn't moved.

Chester was still holding the game puck as they hoisted him onto their shoulders.

"I knew you could do it!" Brady said proudly to his friend. His friend — and the Icehogs' *great* goalie.